Sidewalk Chalk

Sidewalk
Chalk
Poems of the City

by **Carole Boston Weatherford**

Illustrations by **Dimitrea Tokunbo**

Wordsong • Boyds Mills Press

To the City Slickers: Daraius, Robbie, Ryan, and Cassidy
— **C. B. W.**

Special thanks to the Stevens crew of Newburgh, New York
(Wiz, Mellow, Misha, Mara, Dédé, Ronnie, and Mister), George Ford,
and Najac Fotogs, Inc. (Jake, Stiles, and Mom "Gibraltar")
—*I love your face*
— **D. T.**

*The artist gratefully acknowledges the following businesses and individuals for
their help: Richard's Barbershop, Pat and George's Restaurant, Personalities Barbershop,
MaryAnne Rauchet and family, George Gould and family, and Bishop and Evangelist Williams
and the Greater Upper Room Gospel Singers.*

Text copyright © 2001 by Carole Boston Weatherford
Illustrations copyright © 2001 by Dimitrea Tokunbo
All rights reserved

Published by Wordsong
Boyds Mills Press, Inc.
A Highlights Company
815 Church Street
Honesdale, Pennsylvania 18431
Printed in China

U.S. Cataloging-in-Publication Data
(Library of Congress Standards)

Weatherford, Carole Boston, 1956-
Sidewalk chalk : poems of the city / by Carole Boston
Weatherford;
illustrations by Dimitrea Tokunbo. — 1st ed.
[32] p. : col. ill. ; cm.
Includes index.
Summary: Poems of city life from the perspective of young people.
ISBN 1-56397-084-8
1. City and town life—Poetry. 2. American poetry. I. Tokunbo,
Dimitrea. II. Title.
811/. 54 21 2001 CIP AC
00-111792

First edition, 2001
Book designed by Jason Thorne.
The text of this book is set in 14-point Usherwood.

Visit our Web site at www.boydsmillspress.com

10 9 8 7 6 5 4 3 2 1

CONTENTS

ON THE CORNER

The shoeshine man pops a cloth
across black wing tips, his face
reflected in polished leather.
As little girls jump double Dutch,
beaded braids swirl and click.
Brothers with time on their hands
croon in three-part harmony,
setting the pace for foot traffic
up and down the sidewalk.
A boy with a boom box heads
for the blacktop to shoot hoops.
At the bus stop, a lady
toting a shopping bag tells me,
"Be careful crossing the street, honey."

SIDEWALK CHALK

Big and bold now, write your name.
Draw an arrow, then take aim
at a puffy heart: "Kim loves Kyle."
Doodling's sure to bring a smile.
How about some tic-tac-toe?
You be *X*; I'll be *O*.
Draw a yellow happy face
or the finish line for a relay race,
a wide, wide river to leap across,
a little circle for beanbag toss,
a bigger circle to play dodge ball.
Trace a shadow ten feet tall.
Make a line for tug-of-war
and signs that no one dare ignore.
Create a sun with a beaming grin,
a great white shark with a giant fin.
Draw a square to make home plate,
a swirly figure eight to skate.
Big and bold now, write your name.
Keep the score for sidewalk games.

EAT AT MOE'S

Crispy, crunchy, golden brown,
Moe's meals are the best in town.
Oil is sizzling; the grill is hot.
Red beans simmer in a pot.
Bacon's frying for BLTs.
Burgers beg for melted cheese.
Lake trout wears a cornmeal coat.
French fries sail in paper boats.
Steak subs cry for onion rings.
Hot sauce fires up chicken wings.
White bread hugs a fried pork chop.
Crushed ice chills a soda pop.
Moe grills hot dogs, hums a tune
as folks chow down at the greasy spoon.

11

STRAYS

Hazel Harris lives alone,
gathers table scraps and bones
for cats and dogs who have no homes.

Hazel Harris cares for strays
week in, week out, and holidays,
serves them food on battered trays.

Hazel loves each alley cat
and scruffy dog with fleas to scratch.
Her backyard gate's a welcome mat.

RUBBER-TIRE GARDEN

A rubber tire yields surprise:
a tiny garden that beautifies
the block with purple pansy blooms
and pink rosebuds.
Such sweet perfume.

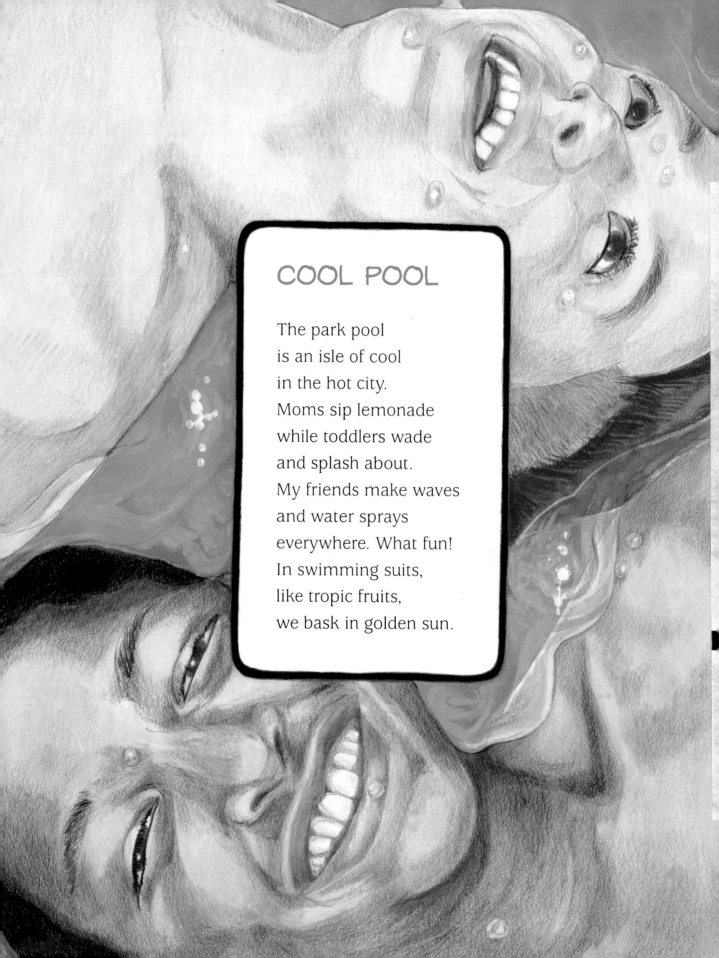

COOL POOL

The park pool
is an isle of cool
in the hot city.
Moms sip lemonade
while toddlers wade
and splash about.
My friends make waves
and water sprays
everywhere. What fun!
In swimming suits,
like tropic fruits,
we bask in golden sun.

CHOCOLATE BUDDIES

We take a break from kickball
when we hear the silvery chime
of the ice-cream truck sounding
its song of summertime.
Coins in pockets jingle
as we hurry down the street,
mouths watering and sweat dripping
in the blazing noonday heat.
I buy some treats for us to share,
two cones, each with a scoop.
How chocolate sweetens friendship
as we chill out on the stoop.

15

ONE RED CENT

On the pavement, there's a penny
somebody surely dropped,
but no one walking by
even takes the time to stop.
Maybe folks would bother
if that red cent were a dime.
I save spare change in a jar;
I'll make that penny mine.

LUCKY NUMBERS

Before Uncle Zeke rises from bed
he checks his dreambook
for lucky numbers to play.
Swears he's gonna win the Lotto.
Last night, I dreamed of my math test.
Wonder if that means I'll get 100?

A CARDBOARD BOX

What can you do with a cardboard box?
Use it to show off your precious rocks.
Build a clubhouse with a door
or a counter for a grocery store.
Make a stage for puppet shows,
a slippery sled for winter snows.
Invent a robot, a high-tech buddy.
Craft a chair to sit and study.
Design a rocket bound for Mars
or turbo-driven racing cars.
Make a sign that says No Boys
or a chest for all your favorite toys.
Don't throw that cardboard box away—
Save it to jazz up a rainy day.

THE LAUNDROMAT

When the Laundromat opens
at seven-thirty,
neighbors pile clothes
that are grimy dirty
into tubs of washing machines
to swoosh around
till the loads are clean.
I change a dollar
for shiny quarters
and pass a washer
that's out of order.
I munch on peanuts
while wet clothes dry.
Mom laughs with friends
and Baby starts to cry.
Mom rests her on the dryer;
Baby hears it hum,
then drifts off to dreamland,
sucking on her thumb.
When the dryer buzzes,
I help my mom fold.
Times like this I kind of wish
I were still three months old.

GROWING ROOM

My room is small.
I share it
with my brothers,
but when I'm snug
beneath the covers,
I'm thankful for
this tiny space—
a room to grow
in love and grace.

BEA THE BEAUTICIAN

I think the beautician
must be a magician.
By the time she was through,
Miz Hooper's hair grew,
Gran's gray hair turned blue,
and my mom looked brand-new.
Oh, the tricks Bea can do.

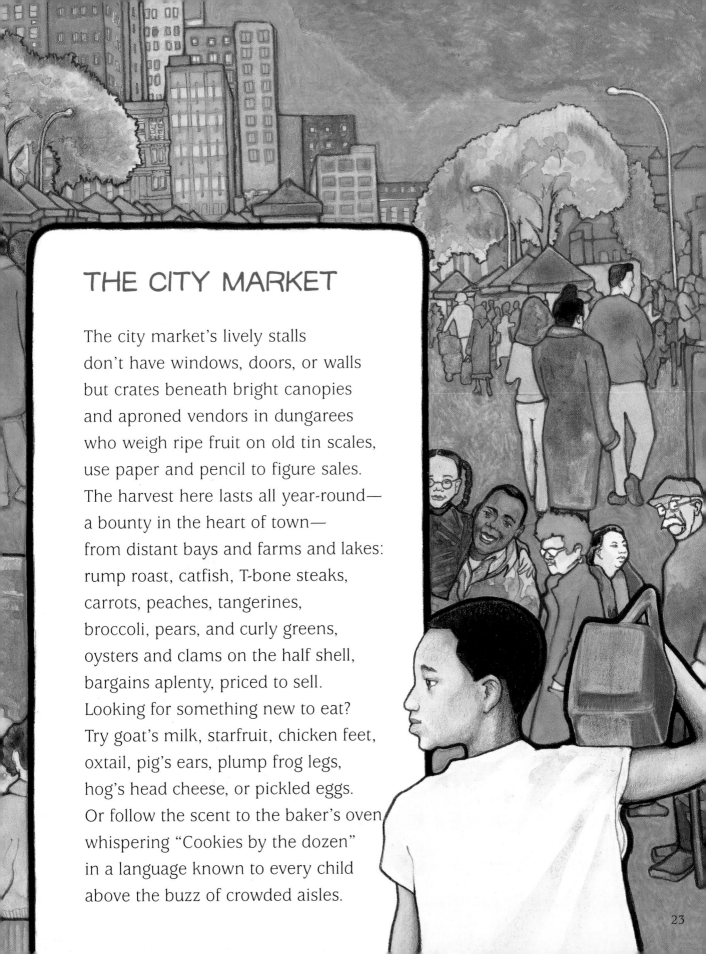

THE CITY MARKET

The city market's lively stalls
don't have windows, doors, or walls
but crates beneath bright canopies
and aproned vendors in dungarees
who weigh ripe fruit on old tin scales,
use paper and pencil to figure sales.
The harvest here lasts all year-round—
a bounty in the heart of town—
from distant bays and farms and lakes:
rump roast, catfish, T-bone steaks,
carrots, peaches, tangerines,
broccoli, pears, and curly greens,
oysters and clams on the half shell,
bargains aplenty, priced to sell.
Looking for something new to eat?
Try goat's milk, starfruit, chicken feet,
oxtail, pig's ears, plump frog legs,
hog's head cheese, or pickled eggs.
Or follow the scent to the baker's oven
whispering "Cookies by the dozen"
in a language known to every child
above the buzz of crowded aisles.

WASH AND WAX

Saturdays, soap bubbles
stream through the gutter
while guys hose down
and polish up cars.
Lather and scrub.
Wax and rub.
"A man," they say,
"gotta take some pride."
I grab a rag,
hear them brag:
"Ladies take a shine
to a fine ride."

AUNT LIZZIE'S PICTURES

Aunt Lizzie's mantel is like a museum. Darling grandkids and distant cousins gaze from photos spanning decades of smiles and celebrations. Sharing the perch are framed *Ebony* covers: Duke Ellington, Muhammad Ali, and General Colin Powell. On the wall hangs Dr. King's portrait printed on a sliver of tree trunk. Aunt Lizzie dusts those pictures every other day and gives each a place of honor. At her house, it's hard to tell where family ends and pride begins.

SO MANY FAITHFUL

So many churches—
storefronts, stone—
sound bells to call
believers home.
Such heavenly voices,
gospel choirs,
rock the pews
set hearts afire.
So many faithful
clap and shout
chase away
blues, fear, and doubt.
Young souls, old saints
find repair
on bended knee
so deep in prayer.

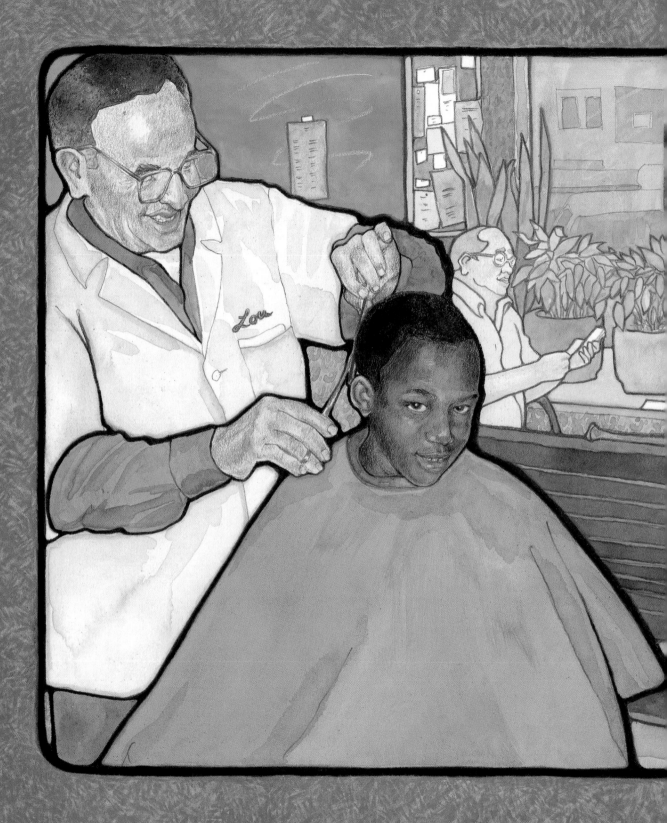

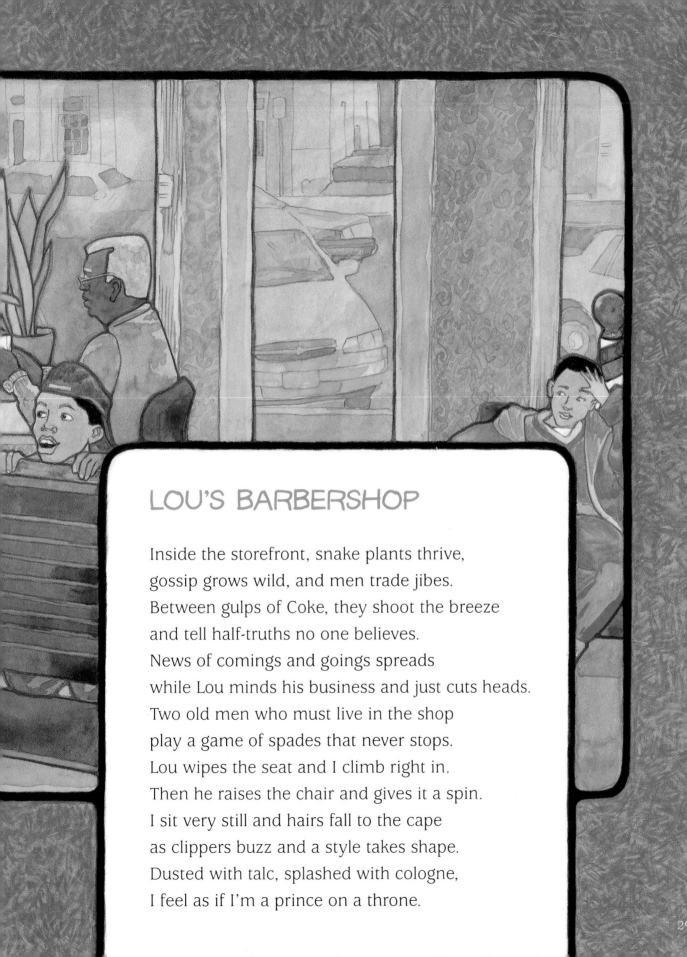

LOU'S BARBERSHOP

Inside the storefront, snake plants thrive,
gossip grows wild, and men trade jibes.
Between gulps of Coke, they shoot the breeze
and tell half-truths no one believes.
News of comings and goings spreads
while Lou minds his business and just cuts heads.
Two old men who must live in the shop
play a game of spades that never stops.
Lou wipes the seat and I climb right in.
Then he raises the chair and gives it a spin.
I sit very still and hairs fall to the cape
as clippers buzz and a style takes shape.
Dusted with talc, splashed with cologne,
I feel as if I'm a prince on a throne.

HAND DANCING

Friday nights, my parents
sing along with golden oldies
on the radio and move
the coffee table to hand dance
in the living room.
Doo-wop shoo-wop ooh ooh.
Mama giggles while Daddy
spins her around. Sitting
out a number on the couch,
they recall their first dance
at a blue-lit house party
years before I was born.
I bet they were really something.

WHERE I LIVE

Where I live
there are no trees
to climb, but I still
reach for the stars.
My dreams take root
in concrete,
and my branches
lift the sky.

31

Index of Titles and First Lines